UP NEXT >>>

:02 SPORTS ZONE SPECIAL REPORT

:04 **FEATURE PRESENTATION:**

SKATEBOARD BREAKDOWN

FOLLOWED BY:

:50 SPORTS ZONE
     POSTGAME RECAP

:51 SPORTS ZONE
     POSTGAME EXTRA

:52 SI KIDS INFO CENTER

LAST YEAR'S SKATING CHAMP, BING HAWTIN, ARRIVES TODAY **SIK** TICKER

SPORTS ZONE
SPECIAL REPORT

SKT
SKATEBOARDING

PNT
PAINTBALL

SNO
SNOWBOARDING

BSL
BASEBALL

BBL
BASKETBALL

HKY

TEEN SKATER STRUGGLES TO COPE WITH TRAGIC LOSS OF HEROIC OLDER BROTHER

TYSON *TAGGART*

STATS:
AGE: 14
NICKNAME: TY

BIO: Ty's older brother, Nick, recently died in service of our country. Ever since then, Ty has been struggling to stay balanced — on his board, *and* in his life. He's skating recklessly, making fans wonder if Ty still has what it takes. But this weekend, we'll find out — Ty will be put to the test against the best of the best, the reigning skatepark champ, Bing Hawtin.

Sports Illustrated KIDS

UP NEXT: SKATEBOARD BREAKDOWN

EDWIN PEREZ

AGE: 21 **JOB:** SOLDIER
BIO: Edwin was Nick Taggart's best buddy in the Armed Forces. He's come to town to visit Ty, hoping to steer the struggling skater back on the right track.

JENNY STEIN

AGE: 15
BIO: Ty's best friend and most loyal supporter. If Ty's competing in a skating contest, Jenny will be cheering him on from the sidelines.

STEIN

BRENDA TAGGART

AGE: 36
BIO: Ms. Taggart is Ty's supportive, strict mother. She takes no bull from Ty, and she keeps him on track and focused on what's important.

MS. TAGGART

JILLY SPEARS

AGE: 19 **JOB:** SKATEPARK OWNER
BIO: Jilly Spears is a patron of the skateboarding art. She regularly hosts competitions and charity drives at her skatepark.

SPEARS

RISING SKATING STAR TY TAGGART HOPES TO DETHRONE FORMER CHAMP,

PRESENTS

A PRODUCTION OF

STONE ARCH BOOKS
a capstone imprint

written by *Eric Fein*
illustrated by *Gerardo Sandoval*
colored by *Benny Fuentes*

designed and directed by *Bob Lentz*
edited by *Sean Tulien*
creative direction by *Heather Kindseth*
editorial direction by *Michael Dahl*

Sports Illustrated KIDS *Skateboard Breakdown* is published by Stone Arch Books,
151 Good Counsel Drive, P.O. Box 669, Mankato, Minnesota 56002.
www.capstonepub.com

Summary: Ty Taggart has always loved skating. But ever since his
older brother, Nick, died in combat, Ty has been off his game. He skates
recklessly and has lost all interest in the local skating tournament. But
when Nick's best friend, Edwin, pays him a visit, Ty is able to reign in
his anger and realize his true skating potential. In the finals, everyone
is dazzled by Ty's slick, flashy tricks — until he wipes out and breaks
his board. Ty will have to pick up the pieces and reassemble his board
overnight if he hopes to prevail.

Cataloging-in-Publication Data is available at the Library of Congress
website.

ISBN: 978-1-4342-2011-0 (library binding)
ISBN: 978-1-4342-2785-0 (paperback)

Printed in the United States of America in Stevens Point, Wisconsin.
032010   005741WZF10

Nick was a soldier. He died in combat six months ago.

It still knocks me off my game.

Ty!
Are you
okay?!

THUD!

Have you gone crazy? Why not? You love skating!

I have to go. Mom said we're having someone over for dinner.

Later, Jen.

Bye, Ty . . .

EISENHOWER ELEMENTARY
MEDIA CENTER
1001 Hwy. 7, Hopkins, MN

Oh man . . . Mom's gonna kill me.

Get cleaned up. Then set the dinner table.

Yes, ma'am.

Mom hasn't been this worried about dinner since Nick came home from basic training.

Hey, bro!

Mom told me you've been getting into trouble since I've been deployed. I just wanted to let you know that I miss you, and I think about you a lot.

You know, life's a lot like a skatepark. It's filled with lots of challenges, like grinds and jumps in a skatepark.

When you're doing a grind, sometimes you lose your balance and wipe out. The trick is to get back up and keep trying until you find your balance.

I know you'll find your balance, Ty.

GRIND ON!

- Nick

I wish. We don't have the money to buy a new skateboard.

No problem . . .

. . . we'll just rebuild yours.

36

Nick and Edwin were right.

I had been out of control.

I needed to find my balance.

46

Life is like a skatepark.

It's full of smooth landings and hard falls.

The trick is to always ... Grind On!

SPORTS ZONE
POSTGAME RECAP

SKT
SKATEBOARDING

PNT
PAINTBALL

SNO
SNOWBOARDING

BSL
BASEBALL

BBL
BASKETBALL

HKY

TAGGART

TY TAGGART GRINDS OUT A PERFECT SCORE TO SEAL THE WIN!

BY THE NUMBERS

FINAL SCORES:
TY: 10.0
BING: 9.9

STORY: Most people expected Ty Taggart to make a decent showing in this year's championship, but few thought the rising star could outshine white-hot skater Bing Hawtin! Sparks flew as the two stellar teens faced off in the final round . . . but once Ty hit his last trick, fans knew there was a new champ in town. Bing Hawtin was quoted as saying, "He may be a little punk, but that Taggart kid sure can grind."

UP NEXT: SI KIDS INFO CENTER

SZ POSTGAME EXTRA

WHERE **YOU** ANALYZE THE GAME!

Skateboarding fans got a real treat today when Ty Taggart one-upped last year's champ, Bing Hawtin, in an amazing skating showdown! Let's go into the stands and ask some fans for their opinions on the day's events ...

DISCUSSION QUESTION 1

Ty wins the skating competition. Have you ever won any competitions? What have you done that you're proud of? Talk about it.

DISCUSSION QUESTION 2

Ty Taggart pulls off tons of tricks in this book. What is your favorite skateboarding trick? Describe it.

WRITING PROMPT 1

Edwin helps Ty during a difficult time in his life. Has anyone lent you a hand when you were feeling down? Write about your helpful experience.

WRITING PROMPT 2

Ty's best friend is Jenny Stein. Who is your best friend? Why are the two of you close? What experiences have you had together? Write about your friendship.

GLOSSARY

360 (THREE-siks-tee)—a trick that involves spinning three hundred and sixty degrees — or a full rotation — in midair

AXLE (AK-suhl)—metal rods that the wheels are connected to

AGGRESSIVE (uh-GRESS-iv)—forceful and fierce

CRITIQUED (kri-TEEKD)—pointed out the good and bad parts

DECK (DEK)—the flat surface of a skateboard

GRIP TAPE (GRIP TAYP)—sandpaper that's placed on the top of the deck. Grip tape provides traction so your feet don't slip.

KICKFLIP (KIK-flip)—a trick where the skater kicks the nose of the board up off the ground and into a barrel roll, then lands back on it

RECKLESS (REK-liss)—careless about safety

TRUCK (TRUHK)—the front and rear axles of a skateboard. The truck connects the wheels to the deck and provides the turning capabilities for the board.

CREATORS

ERIC FEIN › Author
Eric Fein is a freelance writer and editor. He has edited books for Marvel and DC Comics, which included well-known characters such as Batman, Superman, Wonder Woman, and Spider-Man. Fein has also written dozens of graphic novels and educational children's books.

GERARDO SANDOVAL › Illustrator
Gerardo Sandoval is a professional comic book illustrator from Mexico. He has worked on many well-known comics, including Tomb Raider books from Top Cow Productions. He has also worked on designs for posters and card sets.

BENNY FUENTES › Colorist
Benny Fuentes lives in Villahermosa, Tabasco in Mexico, where it's just as hot as the sauce is. He studied graphic design in college, but now he works as a full-time colorist in the comic book industry for companies like Marvel, DC Comics, and Top Cow Productions. He shares his home with two crazy cats, Chelo and Kitty, who act like they own the place.

BING HAWTIN, TY TAGGART, and MATTY LYONS IN:
SKATEBOARD SONAR

MAR 2 3 2002

North Kingstown Library
100 Boone Street
North Kingstown, RI 02852
(401) 294-3306